THE PRIZE

A Collection of Stories

by Flavia Weedn

D0169421

Roserich Designs, Ltd.

Carpinteria, California

In memory of my mother
who taught me
to love

and

my uncle Jack
who taught me
to see

Contents

A LIFETIME

I remember reading in school
    about some great
    historical figure
    who spent a lifetime
    seeking his fortune.

And about a famous
    somebody else
    who spent a lifetime
    doing good deeds.

So when I was ten
    I thought a lifetime
    meant the length of time
    spent on the years
    from birth 'til death.

    That its value was measured
    by the important things
    that happened
    during those years.

    And the only valuable lifetimes
    were those found
    in library books.

When I was twenty
   I was impatient with life
   and with time
   so most of my days
   slipped by
   unnoticed.

   I reached out
   for tomorrows
   trying for a glimpse
   or a touch
   of what my lifetime
   might bring.

I found by my thirtieth year
    that life had brought me pain
    but mingled with it
    was all the joy I'd found.

    Life had been kind
    to me
    for it had not
    left me
    untouched.

A part of me
    thought my lifetime
    was spent.
    The rest of me
    kept pushing
    for what most surely
    would happen
    tomorrow.

    But that was then.

Today I looked at tidepools
      and seabirds
      and found an ageless rock
      washed smooth and grey
      by the sea.

      I sat on the sand
      with my friend
      and shared thoughts
      and tuna sandwiches
      and the sun.

      I gave corn chips
      to a seagull
      and watched him smile.

My friend and I walked
    and talked
    and looked
    at people
    and into
    store windows.

We saw beautiful birds
in handmade cages
and I remembered
the seagull.

My friend told me
    of faraway places
    and we laughed
    and bought
    Christmas tree ornaments.

    I listened closely
    to the words of a song
    that he sang
    about a poem
    written on the back
    of a leaf
    and about a key
    to a house
    with no door.

At a street corner
   we shared
   the discovery
   of a flower
   growing
   deep inside
   a drain.

Souvenirs, all.

When I was ten
how could I
have known
that a lifetime
has nothing to do
with years...

...only with time.

And that its value
isn't measured by
the important things
that happen...

...unless
smiling
with a seagull
is important.

A lifetime?
I spent one
today
with my friend.

◆　◆　◆

Fountain Valley, CA.
July 1975

THE PLAYGROUND

I saw a playground
   today
   deserted and empty
   except for one old man.

   He sat very still
   and to some
   he would have been
   unnoticed.

To the left of the swings
    stood a free-standing
    sculpture
    made for children
    to climb on.

    But it was so perfectly
    perfect
    I suspected it would
    have been happier
    somewhere else.

The sun was so warm
and so bright
it played tricks
through the leaves.

It made me want to run
and hang by my knees
on the bars
and hide
in the tunnel
and pretend.

It was early afternoon
and children
belonged there.

I sat on the grass
and wondered why
the sight
of an empty playground
bothered me so.

The old man
     had not moved
     since I first saw him.
     With bent back
     he just sat on the bench
     and stared into space.

He looked so very alone
my heart remembered
a part of a poem
about the last leaf
upon a tree.

He turned his head slightly
    but enough
    and I could see
    he was smiling
    and he wasn't alone
    at all.

His old friends were there
    young again
    running
    and shouting
    playing
    and pretending.

He was out there
    playing among them
    young like they
    and filling each moment
    with something new.

    All of them
    were laughing
    and playing at life
    like a game.

Spellbound
    I watched
    as the playground
    became older
    and different.
    The magic
    I was seeing
    was all for free.

I heard the squeaking
    of swings
    and the scuffling
    of feet.
    The children were all
    around me
    so close
    we could touch.

The sounds in the playground
 grew louder
 and my eyes flashed
 from the old man
 to the children
 then back again
 to the sun
 in the trees.

Suddenly
    the old man
    stood up
    and my symphony
    was over
    as abruptly
    as it had begun.

I watched him
pick up his cane
and slowly
walk away.

It was I
     who was motionless
     now
     and alone
     and the only sound
     in the playground
     was the pounding
     of my heart.

I looked
     at the fallen leaves
     that had scattered
     around me
     and those
     still clinging
     to the trees.

     I was strong
     with the feeling
     that I had stepped
     into someone else's
     dream.

As he walked away
    the old man
    never looked back.
    Not once.
    But there was
    no need.
    He knew.

    His friends
    would be there
    waiting
    in the playground
    whenever
    he needed them.

               ◆   ◆   ◆

Fountain Valley, CA
September 1975

TWIGS

The calendar
   claimed November
   but summer
   had designed the day.
   We drove
   along the coast
   my mother
   and I.
   Both marveling
   at the people
   who could steal time
   from Wednesdays
   to sit on the beach.

Maybe it was the magic
of the California sun
or the surfers
or the hot dog signs
but an hour later
as we walked
along the sidewalks
even the store windows
and the city signs
couldn't make me think
of anything beyond
how golden and how warm
the day.

But once we had
    entered the store
    and closed
    the big wooden door
    behind us…
    …quite abruptly
    all signs of summer
    had disappeared.

Strangely and suddenly
we were standing
in a world
filled with Christmas.

The air
    was actually
    a winter's chill
    and heavy with the scent
    of pine and of maple
    of cinnamon sticks
    and the earthy potpourri
    smells of Christmas.

Christmas trees
   stood tall and proud.
   Each one
   reaching
   for the high wooden beams
   of the ceiling.
   Each one
   heavily adorned
   with bangles and beads
   wooden figures
   and fabric fancies
   tiny toys
   and silver bells.

   Each one
   selling Christmas.

The glass ornaments
    made twinkling rainbows
    on the walls
    and the shines
    and shadows
    made each tree aware
    as they competed
    in their silent beauty pageant.

The hum of people's conversations
        mixed together
        with the sounds
        of many footsteps.
        Decisions of what to buy
        for whom
        were overshadowed
        by the beauty
        that engulfed the room.

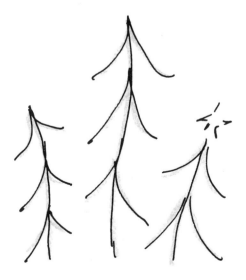

My mother and I
    became part
of the crowd.
Very like
everyone else.
A little lost
in the magic
of the room
and in our own
personal reflections
of Christmases past.

When we left the store
	and walked to the car
	we each carried
	one of the store's
	white printed bags.
	Each filled with remnants
	of the Christmas we'd found.

	Inside mine
	carefully wrapped
	in tissue
	was a gift for her.
	And in my mother's
	a gift for me.

On the quiet ride back
we relaxed.
My mother mentioned
how hot
the late afternoon sun.

I noticed
the stragglers
lingering
on the beach.

As the road turned
    away from the coast
    toward home
    the eucalyptus trees
    appeared
    on our right.

The silouettes
of their blue-grey forms
stood in all their glory
against the burnt-orange
of the sky.

But…up close
    their shapes seemed
    tired and old
    like forgotten people
    standing
    lonely
    in
    an
    empty
    field.

I stopped the car
when we saw
the piles of dried
branches and boughs
that had fallen
from the trees.

They lay grey and still
as they beckoned through
the patterned streaks
of sunshine
that spread over them
on the ground.

We began
    to gather
    great bunches
    of twigs...
    ...my mother
    and I.

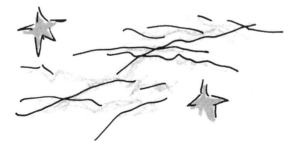

Two women
ankle deep
in broken leaves
and branches.

Two women
     stumbling
     and giggling
     in soft grey dirt
     by the side
     of a busy highway…
     …filling our arms
     and then the trunk
     of the car
     with dusty twigs.

Time eluded us.

We were
       children again
       as we stepped over
       and reached through
       and laughed
       while bits of
       the twigs
       we gathered
       clung to our clothing.

While
    we loaded the car
    we spoke
    of wrapping
    bunches of twigs
    with giant cloth ribbons
    and giving them
    as Christmas gifts…

    …gifts of
    gathered firewood
    to burn
    on Christmas Eve.

Whatever
Christmastime
magic that each of us
had personally
felt as children
had returned.

I watched my mother's face
and saw
how her eyes
belied her age
as they
smiled back
at me.

I felt
a surge of warmth
within me
when I realized
that for these
few moments
in time
we had managed
to melt years away.

We were
        as two young friends
        sharing
        the spontaneity
        of a rare
        and beautiful
        experience…
        …and
        without opening
        any store tissue
        or printed paper bags
        we were exchanging
        gifts with each other.

We had found
    Christmas…
    …my mother
    and I.

Not in that shiny store
but here and now
in this field.

And these gifts
 to each other
 we would keep
 forever...
 ...for they
 were not found
 in the twigs...

 ...but in
 the gathering.

   ◆ ◆ ◆

Fountain Valley, CA
November 1975

THE SOUND OF TUESDAY

A voice on the radio
    said a helicopter crashed
    this afternoon
    in Burbank.

Two fatalities.

It seems much colder today.
    Wished my heater worked.
    My plants seem brighter
    change in the weather
    I guess.
    Winter must be here.

    I wonder
    if their families
    have been notified
    by now.

My painting is almost finished.
　Shoulders ache.
　Getting hungry.
　Should start dinner soon.

　The people across my courtyard
　are laughing
　loudly
　and listening
　to an opera.
　Too loud.
　Hard to concentrate.

Local police
    report a thirty year old
    Long Beach woman
    accidentally shot in the head
    by her roommate
    at two o'clock today.
    Died en route
    to local hospital.

Thirty years old.

I was pregnant when I was thirty.

Everything from my window
   looks so still.
No wind
no seagulls
just the silent sand.
The only movement
is in the sky.
The sun is setting
and the clouds
are changing colors.

I wonder if she had a child.

There's that sad old dog
    with that frightened face.
    Body moving straight ahead
    eyes darting from side to side.
    Desperately looking
    for someone
    somewhere.
    Unaware
    he's going
    nowhere.

My neighbor upstairs
is exercising again.
Jogging in place
on his floor
on my ceiling.

A five car collision
    has just occurred
    southbound
    on the Santa Ana Freeway
    near Atlantic Blvd.
    Rush hour traffic
    is snarled
    backed up as far as Soto Street.
    Wreckage covers three lanes.

    Highway patrol
    and three ambulances
    are rolling.

Motorists
    are advised to use
    alternate routes
    for approximately
    two and a half hours.
       REPEAT
    Motorists
    are advised to use
    alternate routes
    for approximately
    two and a half hours.

Lisa is sad today.
    She cried
    because her goldfish died.
    I'm glad.

    Not because
    her goldfish died
    but because
    she cares
    and she's eighteen years old
    and not ashamed to cry.

Bellflower police
     report a young man
     stabbed to death
     in a local trailer park.
     Clad in T-shirt
     jeans
     and tennis shoes.
     The youth was found
     at 6:35 this AM
     in Space 317
     where he lived
     alone.

He was twenty-one.

Now the courtyard people
    are playing James Taylor.
Softer.
Easier to paint by.

Rick is almost twenty-one.

There was
no apparent motive
for the crime.

A spokesman for Disneyland
    expects record breaking
    attendance
    for the approaching
    Christmas season.

Did you know
    that three out of five
    children
    alive today
    will go to bed
    hungry
    tonight.

The outside stillness
   is broken by
   a siren.
   It is loud
   and
   very
   clear.

Delta is ready when you are
wherever you want to go.

The day is ending
 I'll finish my painting
 tomorrow.
 Need to walk
 on the sand
 and be by the ocean
 now.

 My friend…
 the ocean.
 Whose sight
 makes me feel new
 and alive
 and a part of
 the awesome mystery
 of life.

*And whose sound
delights me
and brings me
peace
and promises
and hope…
…always hope
for tomorrow.*

And Datsun saves.

♦ ♦ ♦

*Sunset Beach, CA
October 1976*

SOMETIMES

Sometimes
    she comes to me
    when my head
    is already so full
    I think
    my mind
    can't handle
    another thought.

Then simply by her presence
　　she has a way
　　of fading away
　　the heavy stuff.

　　Maybe that's why
　　she chooses those times
　　to come to me.
　　Or do I
　　choose those times
　　to let her in.

　　Is she my escape?

She took much with her
    when she first went away.
    Sometimes
    I think she took
    more than she left
    behind.

    Her disappearance was slow
    and gradual
    and now
    I suspect
    no one ever sees her
    but me.

I've given away
  some of what she gave me
  to my children.

    They
    who never knew her
    share her sensitivity
    her vulnerability
    and her deep love
    of being.

Her most personal things
I've kept for myself.
Some leftover dreams
and a handful
of hopes
that died too young.

Sometimes
    I can see clearly
    the print of her
    high school graduation dress.

Or hear
    the Hoagy Carmichael song
    that was playing
    the first time
    she fell in love.

I can remember
    sometimes
    the dumb things
    she used to do
    and now they make me
    smile.

    And the warm times
    when she and I
    are very alone
    together
    and I realize
    how easy it is
    for her to make me
    cry.

Most of my days
　　　are very crowded now
　　　and I forever hurry.
　　　Even my time shared
　　　with her
　　　is hurried.

　　　But it's time
　　　I need
　　　for it is necessary
　　　to look back
　　　and touch her
　　　sometimes
　　　just so she can see
　　　where I am going.

There are times
    she seems just beyond
    my sight
    and I can only imagine
    the look
    of her face
    of her hands…

    …and the pure
    and beautiful
    UNCOMPLICATEDNESS
    of her life.

I wonder
   if she knows
   how much
   I miss her...

      ....sometimes...

...this girl
that I used to be.

♦   ♦   ♦

Sunset Beach, CA
October 1976

THE GIFT

Someone stole my car
   last night.
   Damn!
   How could they?
   I feel empty.
   No, more than that
   I feel offended
   and violated
   and angry.

Kind:
    VW Karmann Ghia
Year:
    1967
    Old.
Color:
    Faded Gold
    Earl Scheib Gold
Plates:
    WBL 226
    Pronounced wobble.

    Had original black plates
    original tool kit
    even original owner's manual.
    Nifty, I thought,
    but nobody asked.

Identification marks:
    None I could list.
    All the marks I could think of
    were those
    no one would understand.

Case number:
    512-183
    The investigating officer
    left his card.
    It read Sheriff-Coroner.

Coroner.
How appropriate.
This is a euology
for a Karmann Ghia.

If whoever took it
    doesn't rub Armor All
    on the dash board
    the leather will crack.
    Karmann Ghias do that
    you know.
    There's some
    in the glove compartment
    with my cologne.

    How stupid!
    My car's been stolen
    and I'm staring out my window
    hoping the thief
    will take care
    of the dash board.

For almost seven months
    I've lived in a small beach house
    whose main source of light
    comes from shuttered windows
    which overlook
    a narrow strip
    of parking
    which overlooks
    a wider strip of sand
    which the ocean overlooks.

Most of these months
    I've spent alone
    or so I thought
    until I realized
    I wasn't.
    I had someone.
    I had me.

    Old habits faded
    new ones were born.
    Began keeping
    my car and house locked.
    Even bought one of those
    chain things
    for my door.

My car was always parked
in the same place
under the street light
first space
from the corner.
The one
that's empty now.
Exactly twelve
steps from car to house.

I know, I counted.
It's one of the
new habits
I had developed.

So there my car has been
       every night
       parked and locked
       just where it belonged.

Then, last night
someone came
and took it.

Its predecessor
        had been a new Porsche 911.
        Expensive and impressive
        fully equipped
        ski rack and all.
        Gorgeously dressed
        in its elegant original
        Porsche Desert Tan Creation.

        No scars, no signs of wear
        only wax
        and gloss.

When I drove the Porsche
I felt wealthy.
Dollar wealthy.
Like the world
was looking
at me.

I justified my soul
with repeated tales
of why
I deserved to own it.

My life had already begun
    to change
    when the Porsche
    was sold.
    And I felt good
    about selling it.
    I would be free
    of the built-in-guilt
    that was slowly surfacing.

Guilt that came
    from owning something
    I truly felt
    extravagant.

And so…
     three months ago
     I bought
     my ten year old Karmann Ghia.
     Found it
     on a dirty and dusty
     vacant lot.

     I knew it would become
     part of my plan
     to simplify
     my life.
     A part of my change of direction
     and search
     for peace of mind.

If there had ever been a doubt
in my head
whether or not
this car was right
for me...
...it disappeared
when I realized
it had no reverse gear.

Significant
you see
because
now
I could
only
go
forward.

It had the look
    of a classic
    waiting
    to be rescued.

    Not a super star classic
    like Kathryn Hepburn
    more of an
    Irene Dunne.

    They don't make them
    anymore
    you see
    so it was like
    finding a rare book
    one out of print.
    I liked the feeling.

What else
        did I leave in the car...
        that research I'd done
        on children's books.
        A sketch pad or two.
        Some drawings.
        Proof sheets of Christmas cards.
        Lisa's shoes
        the straw ones.
        A box of Kleenex
        white.
        My sun glasses
        and a Bic pen
        fine line.

        Oh Lord, something HAS died.
        I've just listed
        the last effects.

I must get things
        into perspective now
        and stop making
        such a big thing
        out of this.
        Cars are stolen all the time.
        It's not like
        losing a loved one.
        It's only a car.
        A material thing.
        Something
        that can be replaced.

        But...it was a loved thing
        and how can I replace
        all that I feel for it.

And tell me…
    how can I replace
    my gold bracelet
    in the side pocket
    or the belt
    to my burgundy dress
    that temporarily
    had become the latch
    that held up the back seat
    or the Indian blanket
    in the back window.

    The old faded one
    I carried Kookie in
    the last time I took her
    to the vet.
    The very last time.

It's not right...it's not!
I want it back!
Why did they choose
my car anyway?
They could see
it had a mushed-in nose
and there was no tape deck
no speakers.
Just an AM radio
and a clock
that didn't run.

It's dark now.
   As I close my shutters
   my parking place
   is still empty
   save for a tossed beer bottle
   which, to the delight
   of my sense of justice,
   shows no reflection
   from the street light.
   All this about a car.
   How ridiculously sentimental
   for allowing myself
   to become so attached
   to a machine.

There must be something good
to come from this.
Somewhere a hidden gift
a lesson learned.

Maybe when my anger subsides
and I have more time
to think about it
I'll know what it is.

And maybe then I'll realize
that nothing can ever
be replaced.
Ever.
Because people
and things
and feelings
don't replace
each other.
They were never meant to.

Each new thing
that comes into our lives
becomes a part of us
and adds
to what we already are
and to what we already feel.

That's the gift
    isn't it.
    Realized now
    at this very moment.
    All the love I felt
    for everything
    in and about that car
    are feelings
    I still have.
    Feelings that are
    a part of me
    a part of what I am.
    My car was never anything
    but a car.

    And a car was all they took.
    They couldn't take away
    my feelings.

Oh Lord,
    by some special miracle
    let me see a car
    parked on that empty
    parking place
    tomorrow morning.
    An ordinary car
    Earl Scheib in color.

    Let it be there
    just long enough
    for me to say thank you...
    ...and to tell it
    that I still have
    all the gifts
    it gave me.

      ◆ ◆ ◆

Sunset Beach, CA
December 1977

THE PRIZE

There's this man
    that I know
    who makes me think
    deep thoughts
    about myself.

It's not that he asks.
He never has.
He doesn't say it
with words.

But there's a look
in his eyes
and a way
that he smiles
that makes me ask myself
questions
inside.

He takes each day
in a simple way.
Some say he has nothing
but then
they see this look
about his face
and know
there's something
special
about this man.

It's as if he's learned secrets
    that very few know
    or holds the key
    to some wisdom
    he's found.

    This same look is shared
    by others
    I've met
    and I know
    each has found it
    alone.

It's not money
    or power
    or position
    he holds…
    …he just celebrates
    being alive.

The merchants
on the streets
who sell their souls
and the frightened ones
who hide inside
could change their lives
if they had what he has
but they stay
on their
merry-go-rides.

Sometimes
    he feels guilty
    I think
    for the way that he lives
    for his contentment just to be
    and to feel.

    Yet he must know
    it's the world
    that he owns
    and all that he has
    is for free.

Like the feel
     of the sand
     on the beach
     when it's warm
     and the nights
     when he touches
     the sky
     and when the songs
     that he finds
     and keeps giving away
     come back
     as a memory.

It's not really a secret
you see
that he's found.
It's something
each of us has.

It gets lost
sometimes
or just covered up
or we think
someone
takes it
away.

So I'll hold on
    to the thoughts
    that he's made me think
    and I'll be unafraid
    to grow.

    For that's step one
    and the first thing
    to learn
    if I want to be
    all I can be.

I'll never know
   all the thoughts
   of this man
   this friend
   who touched my life.

   Because one day
   he'll leave.
   He'll just go away
   and I'll never see him again.

But he touched my mind
        and I now know
        inside
        that I too
        know the truths
        that he's found.

That TO LIVE
  is the game
    and I've already won...

...because LIFE
LIFE itself...

...is the prize.

•   •   •

Sunset Beach, CA
July 1976

Flavia Weedn's work expresses the basic excitement, simplicity and beauty she sees in the ordinary things of life. Illustrations of soft lines and color complement her editorials, and together communicate a feeling of hope to the human spirit.

Named after a princess in the novel, "The Prisoner of Zenda", Flavia's experiences as a child brought her to a keen awareness of the need for people to express their feelings.

Her professional career forced a choice between fine art and the tailoring of ideas to fit the "greeting card" genre. She has managed to satisfy the demands of both fields, simultaneously winning praise for her paintings and selling millions of her cards by using her works "to let people know it's alright to feel and to show it." As a result, an everwidening audience is discovering Flavia and her ability to put into words what so many feel with their hearts.

Recently, her work has found appropriate homes with other media. Porcelain figurines, ceramic mugs, plates, tiles and bank checks have all found a unique human distinction in Flavia.

Flavia is a person helping others to share her awe of life; such thoughtfulness will never go out of style.

If you wish to know more about Flavia, please write:

The Flavia Collectors' Club
PO Box GG
Carpinteria, California 93013

Roserich Designs, Ltd.
PO Box 1030
Carpinteria, California
93013

Library of Congress Cataloging
in Publication Data

THE PRIZE
A Collection of Stories
Printed in the United States of America
ISBN 0-913289-00-0